SUPER MONSTERS™

MONSTER MASH
A HALLOWEEN STORY

Adapted by Jenne Simon

SCHOLASTIC INC.

Copyright © 2019 Netflix
Netflix Official Merchandise

All rights reserved. Published by Scholastic Inc., *Publishers since 1920.* SCHOLASTIC and associated logos
are trademarks and/or registered trademarks of Scholastic Inc.

The publisher does not have any control over and does not assume any responsibility for author or third-party websites or their content.

No part of this publication may be reproduced, stored in a retrieval system, or transmitted in any form or by any means, electronic, mechanical, photocopying,
recording, or otherwise, without written permission of the publisher. For information regarding permission, write to Scholastic Inc.,
Attention: Permissions Department, 557 Broadway, New York, NY 10012.

ISBN 978-1-338-35496-6

10 9 8 7 6 5 4 3 2 1   19 20 21 22 23

Printed in the U.S.A.   40
First printing 2019

Book design by Marissa Asuncion

Everyone at Pitchfork Pines Preschool shivered with excitement. The Super Monsters were throwing a spook-tacular Halloween carnival for the whole town!

It was almost sunset.

Sun down . . . Monsters up!

Super Monsters!

A little magic and a whole lot of monster style put everyone in the mood to party.

But no one else in Pitchfork Pines had the Halloween spirit!
Where were the decorations and costumes and candy and spooky tricks?
The Super Monsters knew what they had to do: use their powers to save Halloween!

Decorations came first. Drac made some petrifying clay bats!

Katya purr-fectly constructed pretty paper cats. *Meow!*
"They're not nearly as handsome as you!" Katya told her cat, Henri.

Cleo wove some super-glittery spiderwebs.

Spike and Lobo worked together to make floaty ghosts.

Zoe was in charge of the jack-o'-lanterns.

And Frankie got some terrifying tunes ready to go. Everyone loved to dance to "The Monster Mash"!

Next, they picked out costumes for everyone in Pitchfork Pines. They found a lion mask, funny rabbit ears, and a pair of superhero outfits. And Spike spotted the perfect pirate costume for their friend Albert.

"Aarrrggggh ye ready for Halloween, mateys?" Spike joked.

Then the Super Monsters delivered
their Halloween surprises around town.
   Katya cast the perfect spell.
*"At every house on every block,
let doorbells ring and knockers knock!"*
   Soon everyone was filled with Halloween spirit!

Everyone except Albert.

"I'm afraid of Halloween," he told the Super Monsters. "It's way too scary for me!"

"But you have to come to the carnival!" said Drac. "It's going to be fang-tastic!"

"There's going to be treats and games and treats and crafts and . . . treats!" said Spike.

"Do you promise it won't be scary?" Albert asked shyly.

The Super Monsters nodded.

Albert agreed to give the carnival a try.

And it turned out to be just as much fun as his friends had promised! There was a beanbag game made with real magic beans. Albert won a prize at the mummy ring toss.

They tried out Frankie's hammer strike game.
Then they watched *Zombie Dance Fever*, a puppet show Zoe's family put on!

Albert was nervous about exploring the hay maze with Lobo. Who knew what waited around every corner?

When an eerie blue glow surprised him, Albert dove behind a haystack.

It was only Zoe, walking through the maze wall.

"Sorry I scared you, Albert!" she said. Zombies liked mazes, but they did them a *little* differently than other people.

And, it turned out, Albert liked mazes, too—especially with his friends by his side.

"Let's go see Drac's haunted classroom next!"
Frankie suggested.

Everyone promised Albert it would be fun and not
too scary.

But *any* scary was too scary for Albert.

The Super Monsters explained that the haunted classroom was just make-believe. They hoped Albert would be brave enough to try it out. "Okay," Albert finally agreed. "I'll do it . . . if you'll stay next to me."

The classroom was full of big scares for little Albert. Spooky fog clouded the darkened room in mystery.

Then Albert heard a noise that made his heart race.

The toy box lid opened and closed, all on its own!

A shiver ran down Albert's back. Was the classroom really haunted?

As he walked by the cubbies, the glow of a ghost stopped Albert in his tracks.

"This is too scary!" he panted. "Let's get out of here!"

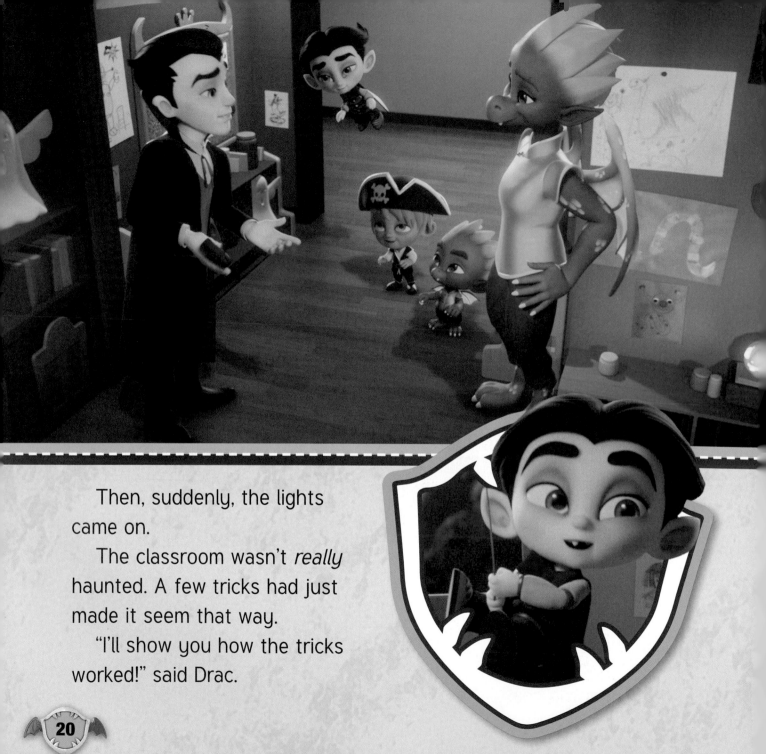

Then, suddenly, the lights came on.

The classroom wasn't *really* haunted. A few tricks had just made it seem that way.

"I'll show you how the tricks worked!" said Drac.

Spike's mother made the fog with her dragon clouds.

Almost-invisible strings opened and closed the toy box lid.

Hidden lights made the ghosts in the cubbies.

And Drac's dad was playing spooky sounds on his phone!

"I think I can understand why people like Halloween," Albert said. And now that he knew how everything worked, he wanted to try the "haunted" classroom again . . . in the dark!

Albert even created a scare of his own. He crept up behind Frankie and . . . "Boo!"

The Super Monsters' Halloween carnival was a spook-tacular success!

Now that they'd had their fill of thrills and chills, Frankie cranked up the tunes.

Everyone busted out their creepiest dance moves.
Frankie smiled and shouted, "Best. Halloween. Ever!"
It seemed everyone in Pitchfork Pines had finally found their Halloween spirit.
Have you?